A Queen's Promise

JS

1075432

First published in 1997 by Franklin Watts
96 Leonard Street, London EC2A 4RH

Franklin Watts Australia, 14 Mars Road
Lane Cove, NSW 2066

Editor: Kyla Barber
Series editor: Paula Borton
Designer: Kirstie Billingham
Consultant: Douglas Ansdell

A CIP catalogue record for this book
is available from the British Library

ISBN 0 7496 2589 9

Dewey Classification 941.105

Printed in Great Britain

A Queen's Promise

by
Kirsty White

Illustrations by Hamesh Alles

W
FRANKLIN WATTS
LONDON • NEW YORK • SYDNEY

Caerlaverock Castle

· 1

A Royal Visit

James was sitting with his father at the
front door of their cottage when Meg, his
sister, came running down the street.

"Guess what?" she said breathlessly.

She'd been with Ma scouring for grain
and was covered with dust from the fields.

James grinned at her. "What?"

"The Queen's coming. Queen Mary! She's been to Dundrennan and she's coming to Dumfries!"

"Away and tidy yourself, girl," said Pa. "You look like a tinker."

Meg scowled and went indoors. Pa did not react to her news at first. James waited for him to say something.

"Ach," Pa said at last, "Mary's just a slip o' a lass."

"She *is* the Queen," James said carefully.

"We need a strong man to lead the country and sort out these devils o'er the border. Yon's a Papist an' all'."

Pa Wallace was a Protestant. He had no time for the Catholics – he said they'd bled the country dry.

Ma came along then, holding a sack half full of grain. Pa stood up and took it from her, then kissed her softly on the cheek.

"You did well, Beth," he said "There's quite a lot here."

Ma shook her head. "Most of it's chaff."

"It'll still make flour."

In the evening, after Pa said grace, the family began to eat. The meal was only a hare that Pa had trapped. There were eight Wallaces and it didn't go far.

"They say Mary's a good woman," Ma said when she'd finished her food.

Pa didn't reply.

"They say she's promised to help us all she can," Ma added.

"I'll believe it when I see it," Pa said stubbornly.

As the sun set the Wallaces all went to bed. There was no money for candles.

James lay awake thinking. He was still hungry after his meagre meal, but it wasn't that. For the past few weeks, the whole family had become used to hunger.

Once, times had been good for the Wallaces. When Pa had the horse and cart, he'd made enough money and the family had wanted for nothing. But Conker had slipped on a cobblestone and broken her leg, and Pa couldn't afford another horse. Ever since, they'd all been struggling.

James was the oldest son. His dearest wish was to help his father, but he didn't know how.

Pa had tried everything to replace Conker. He'd tried to borrow the money, but nobody had any to lend him.

Even Lord Maxwell, the richest man in the region, wouldn't help. He said he'd no money because of what the English had stolen, although the raids had been years ago, long before James was born.

It was all so unfair. Pa was a good man, and he worked very hard. If Pa was right, the new Queen wouldn't help. But Ma said that she'd promised to.

James fell asleep, still thinking about Conker and wondering if the Queen would help them.

2

No Pie for Dinner

Meg woke James before dawn.

"What are you doing?" he whispered.

"Ssshh," she hissed. "I'm going to see the Queen."

"She's not coming till later."

"I'm going to wait for her on the road.

That way, I'll get a chance to see her right up close."

James sat up and tried to shrug off his tiredness. If Meg was going, he'd better go too, because if she went by herself she'd get into trouble. And maybe she was right – if they waited for the Queen on the outskirts of town, he might get a chance to ask her to help them.

Outside the air was chill. James began to run to get warm.

"Wait for me," Meg cried. She had her shawl wrapped around her, but James had outgrown last year's jumper and he had only a shirt on.

They walked down to the river and
crossed it at the bridge. From the top of the
hill on the other side, James could see for
miles, but there was no sign
of the royal party.

"Told you so," he said.

Meg sat down on a stone. "I'll wait."

"I'm off to fish," said James. He had
his hook and line with him – maybe the
Queen's visit would bring him luck.

Meg peered back at the town. It was just a dark shadow nestling in the valley beneath the brilliant light of sunrise.

"It disnae look so bad from a distance," she said as James started to go back down the hill.

James shrugged. Dumfries still bore the scars of the fires started by the English. If Queen Mary saw how bad things were, perhaps she'd do something about it.

James walked along the riverbank until he reached a deep pool, then he baited his line with a worm and settled down to wait.

As the minutes passed, James thought again about a horse. If he had his way, he'd just slip over the border and take one. The English had raided Dumfries again and again under King Henry, and they'd got clean away with it. They wouldn't miss a single horse and it would serve them right for what they'd done. The trouble was, when Pa found out, he'd skelp James for his pains. The Bible said that stealing was wrong and, because the Bible said so, so did Pa Wallace.

Pa also said that God would punish the English for the raids, but James thought that God was taking an awfully long time to get around to it.

By the time the sun was high in the sky, not a single fish had bitten. James had stopped thinking about stealing a horse. He was thinking instead about the Queen's promise. He wondered what sort of person she really was.

He was thinking so hard that he didn't notice the tug at first. By the time he felt it and pulled the line in, the fish had escaped. Never mind her promise, he thought. Queen Mary hadn't brought him any luck.

Tired of fishing, James got up from the riverbank. He could see Meg at the top of the hill, so he walked up along the road a little further, wondering how long she would stay here, with her eyes fixed on the horizon.

Just then James noticed a bramble bush full of ripe and juicy berries. He went to pick some, using a bit of sacking to carry them in.

"Meg, come and help me," he yelled.

Meg ignored him. She was peering into the distance.

"Come on," James shouted irritably.

Meg didn't move. James picked all the ripe brambles. Then, with the full bundle in one hand and the fishing rod in the other, he climbed back up the hill.

"Let's go home," he said. Maybe Ma had some honey put by – she definitely had a little flour. James's stomach rumbled at the thought of a bramble pie.

"Shut up," Meg said. "I can see her."
Sure enough, in the distance, James
saw a big party on horseback. It was too
far away to see who they were, but it had

to be someone very important.

Meg began to run towards them. James ran behind her, scared that she'd fall down in front of the horses and get hurt or, in her excitement, say something rude.

As the riders came closer, he saw that three or four were women, riding side-saddle. At the front was a pale young woman with dark hair. She wore a yellow dress with a stiff lace collar, a ruff and a golden chain with a cross studded with deep ruby stones that flashed in the sunlight. James knew this must be the Queen.

He gathered his courage and moved forward to talk to her. But just at that moment, Meg stepped in front of him and reached out to touch Queen Mary's beautiful dress. James gulped but the Queen just smiled.

"Hello," she said. "Who are you?"

"M-m-m-meg," Meg mumbled.

"Hello, Meg. I'm Queen Mary," the Queen said.

"I'm James," James began to say, just
as a man on horseback behind the Queen
said gruffly that they couldn't stop because
they were already late.

The horses set off at a canter with
the two children running after them.
They chased the royal party all the way
to the river.

As the horses splashed through the mud
Meg and James got soaked to the skin. On
the other side, a crowd was waiting, jostling
each other in their eagerness to see the
Queen. Meg nearly got knocked down in
the crush and James had to pick her up
and carry her to safety. He couldn't even
see the Queen among all the people.

It was the middle of the afternoon when
they got safely back to the cottage.

Meg's eyes were still wide with wonder.

"Wasn't Mary beautiful? Her dress
was as soft as a feather."

James smiled
despite his
disappointment.
"Come on,"
he said, "we'll
have a bramble
pie for dinner."

It was then that he realised that in the crowd the bundle of brambles had been squashed into a sticky mess. All that was left were pips and juice that dribbled down his legs, staining his trews. James was so disappointed he could've cried.

"I'm sorry," he said. He felt the whole expedition had been a waste of time.

But Meg was thinking of something else. Her face fell.

"Oh Mary's dress, her lovely dress. It was all covered with mud around the hem!"

Meg didn't understand about the horse, and about how much Pa needed one.

28

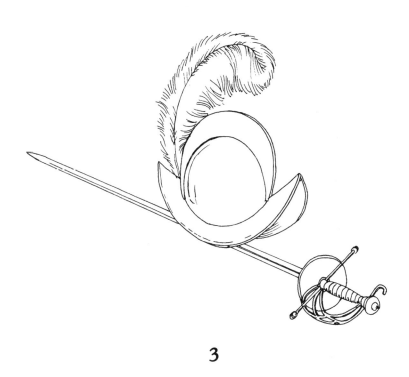

3

James Has a Bright Idea

James lay awake in the darkness, his stomach groaning. They'd only had bread for dinner, and he'd only taken a little as he felt so bad about the brambles.

He turned over and closed his eyes, but sleep did not come.

Round the table, his parents were
talking in whispers.

"You're so grumlie," Ma said to Pa, "I
wish I could cheer you."

"I ken," Pa replied, "we've got to have
faith that the Lord will provide."

"They say Mary's a good woman,"
Ma said again, but Pa said nothing.

James thought of Mary's procession,

the loaded carts that followed her, the
spare horses that followed them. Ma never
talked nonsense, and she believed in the
Queen.

He waited until Ma and Pa fell asleep
and then he got up and slipped outside.
Caerlaverock Castle rose darkly against
the sky, its shape reflected in the dark
waters of the moat.

Lord Maxwell's sentries stood at the gatehouse, arms folded, pikes ready. There were more sentries by the stables, sitting with Mary's guards and drinking ale.

At first James's plan wasn't to steal one of Mary's horses, but to borrow one for a while to give his father a chance to earn enough money to buy one of his own. Mary had so many that she wouldn't miss just one, and he intended to give it back as soon as he could.

But the townspeople were nosy. They'd

want to know where Pa Wallace got his
new horse. So would Pa himself,
come to that.

Taking a deep breath, James
marched up to the gatehouse.

"Please," he said to
the guard, "can you
take a message to
Queen Mary?"

The guard looked
down at him.

"Whit would a
limmer like ye
be wanting wi'
Her Majesty?
Now awa'
afore I
skelp ye!"
the guard
roared.

James slunk away and hid in the rushes by the moat. He'd find a way to talk to the Queen, he was sure of it.

The castle was lit by many candles, and he could hear the sound of music and singing coming from inside. He'd been to the castle once before, after Conker broke her leg, when Pa went to see if Lord Maxwell would lend him another horse. James had felt Pa's pride, and his shame when the lord said abruptly that he couldn't afford to – he was still struggling to make up for the ravages of King Henry. The light of the candles alone proved the lie – the lord was a wealthy man, despite his complaints.

The water in the moat wasn't as deep as James remembered. The summer had been long and dry. He put his foot in and touched the bottom.

Gasping in the chill water, he paddled out until he reached the middle, where the bottom fell sharply away. Muttering a prayer, James plunged forward and then he sank, thrashing wildly against the bottom.

Unable to see anything, he struck out in panic, almost blacking out before he touched a rock and managed to pull himself to the surface on the other side.

Gasping for breath, he clambered out of the moat and lay on the ledge like a landed fish. When he recovered, he looked up and saw that the castle walls rose straight up in front of him without a crack, never mind a foothold.

James's heart sank. There was no way in and no way back either, unless he crossed the moat again.

He was trapped.

4

Never Give Up

The sentries had heard James's panicked splashing. They prowled around the edge of the moat, searching for whatever had caused the noise. James lay still, holding his breath. The moat water was stagnant – it was a wonder they didn't smell him.

"Must have been a duck," said
one sentry
"Aye," said the other.

James gulped air and then, when
they'd gone, he stood up and began to
creep around the walls along the ledge.
The stone was damp and covered with
moss and he slipped several times, but
each time he managed to save himself.

The ledge stopped
at the turret, where
the waters of the
moat lapped
against the walls.

There was no way forward, the water was
black and very deep, the stone covered
with slime.

James wondered if he could make it back across the moat, or if he'd drown in the attempt.

The castle walls seemed to sneer at him, but as he gazed at them, he saw the dents and grazes left by the English cannons. One, just out of reach, was deep enough to grip and above it there were more.

James jumped and missed. He jumped again and

this time he managed to grip the stone and
pull himself up until he found a foot-hold.
Inch by inch, he clawed his way up the wall
of the castle. He looked down just once but
not again because he was afraid of falling.

The turret had no
windows that he could
climb into, only slits
for archers.

At last he reached
the top. As he swung
his leg over, he heard
sentries talking.

James froze.

One of the sentries came over, just along from where James hung by one leg with the other one dangling.

"All quiet," the sentry said.

James prayed. "Please, God, forget the horse, just let me get out of this with my life."

The sentry moved away.

James swung his other leg over and fell down into the shadow of the low wall that surrounded the roof. As the sentries talked, he edged towards a trapdoor. When their backs were turned, he opened it and jumped blindly, landing hard on the floor below.

James rubbed his bumps and then crept down the stairs until he stood in a passage close to the hall where the music was coming from. As maids and footmen bustled past with trays of food and wine, he hid behind a hanging tapestry.

James waited, his mouth watering, his stomach rumbling so loudly that he was afraid that it would give him away. As long as he stayed hidden, he was safe. Lord Maxwell was proud of boasting that the castle's walls had never been breached. He was so confident, in fact, that there was almost no security inside at all.

At last the music ended, and the Queen swept past with her ladies. James waited for a moment more and then he followed them to the door of the room Mary had gone into. He pushed it open very gently.

A strong hand grasped him by the scruff of his neck.

James turned round to find one of Mary's ladies glaring at him.

"Just what are you up to, young man?" she demanded.

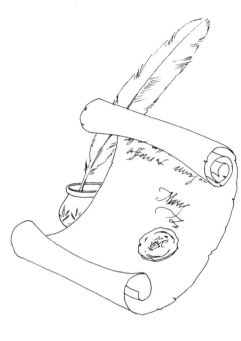

5

James Makes his Plea

"Please," James said, "I just want to talk to the Queen."

"Talk to the *Queen*? Away with you," the lady said. "The cheek of it!"

"Please," James blurted "Ma said the Queen promised to help us and we need her help. We really do!"

"Away with you, or I'll call the guards!"

James stood there defiantly. He'd come so far, he wasn't going to leave with nothing.

"Please," he said again. "I really need to see the Queen."

The lady began to speak, but Queen Mary silenced her with a shake of her head.

"I'll see the lad," she said.

"But, ma'am, he might be dangerous."
The Queen shook her head again.
"I'll call if I need you," she said.

The Queen led James into her room and told him to sit down.

"What is it that you want?" she asked.

Now that he had actually reached her, James wasn't sure what to say.

The Queen looked at him closely. "Aren't you the boy I saw on the road today? With the little girl called Meg?"

"Yes," James said. "Meg's my sister. I'm James."

The Queen smiled. "Well, James, why are you here?"

All of a sudden, it didn't seem like such a good idea. James's face turned red. He would have run away, except then he'd have to face the sentries.

"I'm the Queen," Mary said, gently, "so it's my job to help you. I promise I will, if I can, but I can't help if I don't know what you need."

James blurted out the story of the horse. He hadn't even got to the point of asking Mary if he could borrow one of hers when she stopped him.

"I've got plenty of horses," she said. "I'll give you one."

"Pa'll pay you back, soon as he makes the money," James said.

Mary shook her head. "There's no need," she said. "I was going to leave one with Lord Maxwell anyway, but you had the courage to ask, so you deserve it."

James was so grateful he nearly cried.

Mary's maid took him to the stables and helped him choose a young mare who'd not only be able to pull his father's cart but would also give him a foal so that he'd never be short of a horse again.

Then she took him back to the Queen, who wrote a letter to his father to explain that the horse was a gift.

James was embarrassed that he could not read. The pastor gave classes after the service each Sunday, but he never paid attention and in any case he could not afford paper or ink. He decided then that he would learn to read and write somehow, even if he had to mark the letters in dust with a stick.

When Mary handed him the letter, James thanked her.

"I'm glad to help," she said.

Mary called her maid and asked her to get James some food. The maid brought a plate of beef and a whole loaf of bread. James ate hungrily.

Mary told him that she knew how poor the country was, and that she wanted to help.

"It's not easy being a queen," she said. "Most of the men don't like it, and they don't like me being a Catholic either. You're not a Catholic, are you?"

James shook his head. "My father's with John Knox."

"John Knox is a very clever man,"

Mary said. "There's
a lot of sense in what he
says. But I don't think
he likes me."

James looked
away. Pa
didn't like
the Queen
much either.

"I wish he'd
give me a chance," Mary said. "There's no
reason why a woman shouldn't run the
country as well as a man. And I don't mind
how people worship, so long as they're with
God and not the devil."

"I-I think you're a good queen," James
stammered.

Mary smiled, and asked him why he
hadn't finished his beef.

James said that he wanted to take it

home with him, because his family had
never tasted fresh beef, only salted.

Mary laughed and told
him to wrap it and the loaf
in the napkin, Maxwell
wouldn't miss it.

James thanked her again, then her maid
took him down to the gatehouse where one of
the Queen's men was waiting with the horse.

Holding the mare's reins, James walked proudly back to Dumfries. Pa was waiting outside the cottage. He saw the horse and then James gave him Mary's letter. Pa read it carefully twice and then he said nothing for a long time.

"You're not angry, are you?" James asked.

Pa shook his head. "I'm thinking I was wrong about the woman."

James gave him the beef and bread. Pa
ate his share and left the rest for the others.

"Maxwell didn't let you into the castle,
did he?"

James took a deep breath and told him
he'd climbed the wall. Pa cuffed him
playfully and told him never to do anything
like that again, because however bad

things were, they would be much worse if
James got hurt. Then he laughed because
Lord Maxwell's boast about the castle was
good no longer.

Ma came to the door and to see what
was going on. When she saw the horse, her
face broke into a huge smile.

Pa told her the mare had come from

the Queen's stables.

"I always said she was a good woman," said Ma.

Meg heard them too. She came out rubbing the morning sleep from her eyes. Pa told her the story. When he finished, she looked at James mournfully.

"Couldn't you have got me a piece of that cloth her dress was made of too?"

Pa looked at James. "There's no pleasing some people," he said with a wink.

Mary, Queen of Scots 1542–1587

Mary became Queen when her
father, King James V, died
when she was only six days old.
She was brought up at the
French court, where she
married the Dauphin Francis
(the heir to the French throne)
at the age of fourteen. She was
widowed two years later.

Mary came to Scotland in 1561, after the
death of her mother.

Mary's life and reign were surrounded by
intrigue and bloodshed. King Henry VIII of
England raided Scotland often when Mary was
an infant, because he was trying to unite the
English and Scottish thrones by marrying her to his
son Edward. She was the first (and only) queen to
reign over Scotland, and she faced opposition
because she was a woman but also because she
was a Catholic.

As an adult, Mary married twice. Her first husband, Lord Darnley (the father of her son James, who went on to become King of both England and Scotland), was murdered. Her second marriage, to the Earl of Bothwell, caused such a scandal that Scottish nobles rebelled. Mary was imprisoned and persuaded to step down from the throne in favour of her baby son James in 1567. Mary escaped a year later and fled to England, where Queen Elizabeth I imprisoned her. Mary was executed in 1587, after she had been accused of being part of a Catholic plot to assassinate Queen Elizabeth.

John Knox (c. 1513–1572)

John Knox was the most important religious leader of his time. He was briefly a Catholic priest, then he trained as a lawyer. He was a passionate preacher and also a good politician.

He wanted to make peace with England and spent a lot of time there, but he had to flee because the English queen Mary Tudor was persecuting Protestants.

Knox frequently criticised Queen Mary for her Catholicism and the fact that she enjoyed dancing. The two met several times and argued vigorously.

Life in the time of Queen Mary

Scotland was a very poor country in the sixteenth century. Most of the people made a meagre living from the land. The wealthy lived in fortified castles, like Caerlaverock Castle in the story. (The castle is

in ruins today. It is six miles outside Dumfries.) Most people could not read or write, although since 1496 there had been a law that made education compulsory for the eldest sons of lairds.

In 1561, when Mary took her throne, the Highlands were ruled by the clan chiefs. The countryside of the borders was populated by gangs called reivers, who made their living by stealing from the English and each other. Only the Lowlands were under the Queen's control, and she faced opposition there from the local lairds, most of whom plotted against her.

The towns and cities (burghs) were governed by councils which were usually appointed by local landowners. The burghs operated courts, which fined criminals and ordered them to compensate their victims. In Dumfries, the town council employed a town orator, a minstrel, ale testers and surveyors who fixed land boundaries. The council also operated a grammar school, and occasionally gave money and help to the poor.

The Scots language

Scots is a dialect that was spoken throughout Lowland and Central Scotland in days gone by. It is still in use today. Much of Scotland's best literature is written in Scots, such as the work of Robert Burns, Robert Henryson, Hugh MacDiarmid and Sir David Lindsay.

Scots developed from the Northern English language spoken by the early Norman settlers. Scots uses words that are based on French, Flemish, Latin and the Scandinavian languages.

Some Scots words are:

drumlie	gloomy
limmer	rogue
skelp	hit
ken	know

Robert Burns